MY 1ST
GRAPHIC
NOVEL®

THE MISSING
MONSTER CARD

MY FIRST GRAPHIC NOVELS ARE PUBLISHED BY STONE ARCH BOOKS
A CAPSTONE IMPRINT
1710 ROE CREST DRIVE
NORTH MANKATO, MINNESOTA 56003
WWW.CAPSTONEPUB.COM

Library of Congress Cataloging-in-Publication data is available on the
Library of Congress website.

Library Binding: 978-1-4342-1888-9
Paperback: 978-1-4342-2284-8

Summary: Ethan can't wait to show Zack his new Monster Card. But when Ethan
can't find the new card, the search for the missing Monster Card begins.

Art Director: BOB LENTZ
Graphic Designer: EMILY HARRIS
Production Specialist: MICHELLE BIEDSCHEID

THE MISSING MONSTER CARD

by Lori Mortensen

illustrated by Rémy Simard

STONE ARCH BOOKS

a capstone imprint

HOW TO READ A GRAPHIC NOVEL

Graphic novels are easy to read. Boxes called panels show you how to follow the story. Look at the panels from left to right and top to bottom.

Read the word boxes and word balloons from left to right as well. Don't forget the sound and action words in the pictures.

The pictures and the words work together to tell the whole story.

Every Saturday, Ethan went to Zack's house. They played Monster Cards for hours.

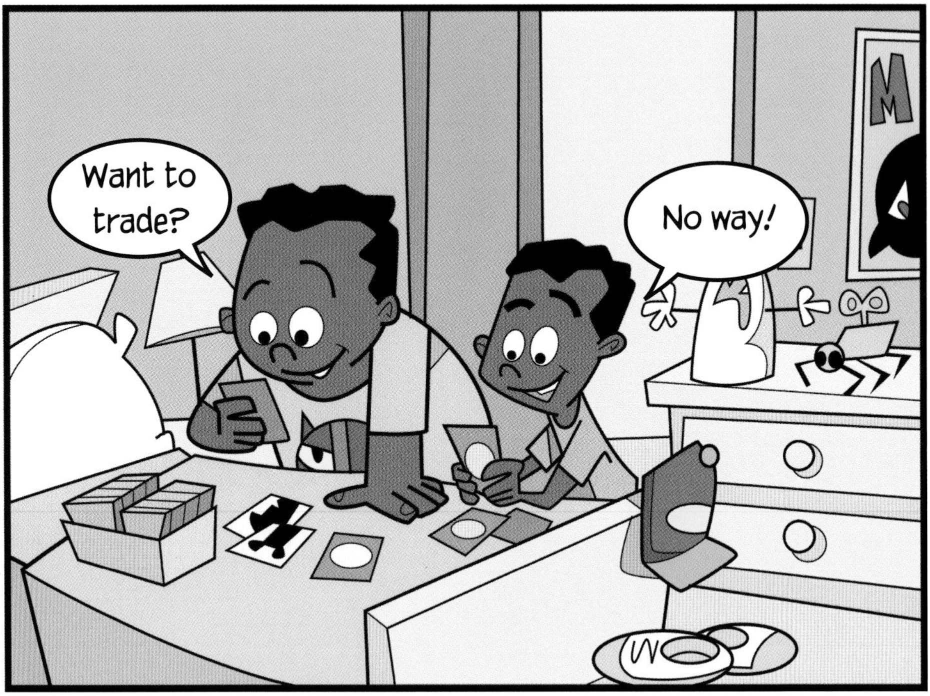
Want to trade?
No way!

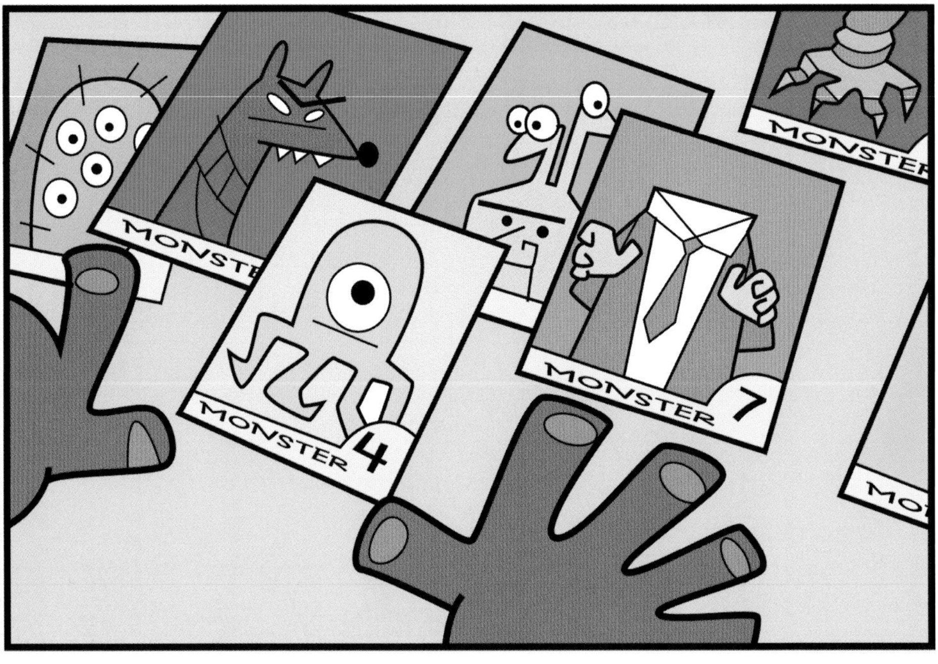
MONSTER
MONSTER 4
MONSTER 7
MONSTER

Ethan couldn't wait for this Saturday. He had a new card. And not just any new card.

The most priceless Monster Card you could get.

That night, Ethan put the card in his coat pocket.

The next morning, Ethan grabbed his coat and called Zack.

He raced to Zack's house.

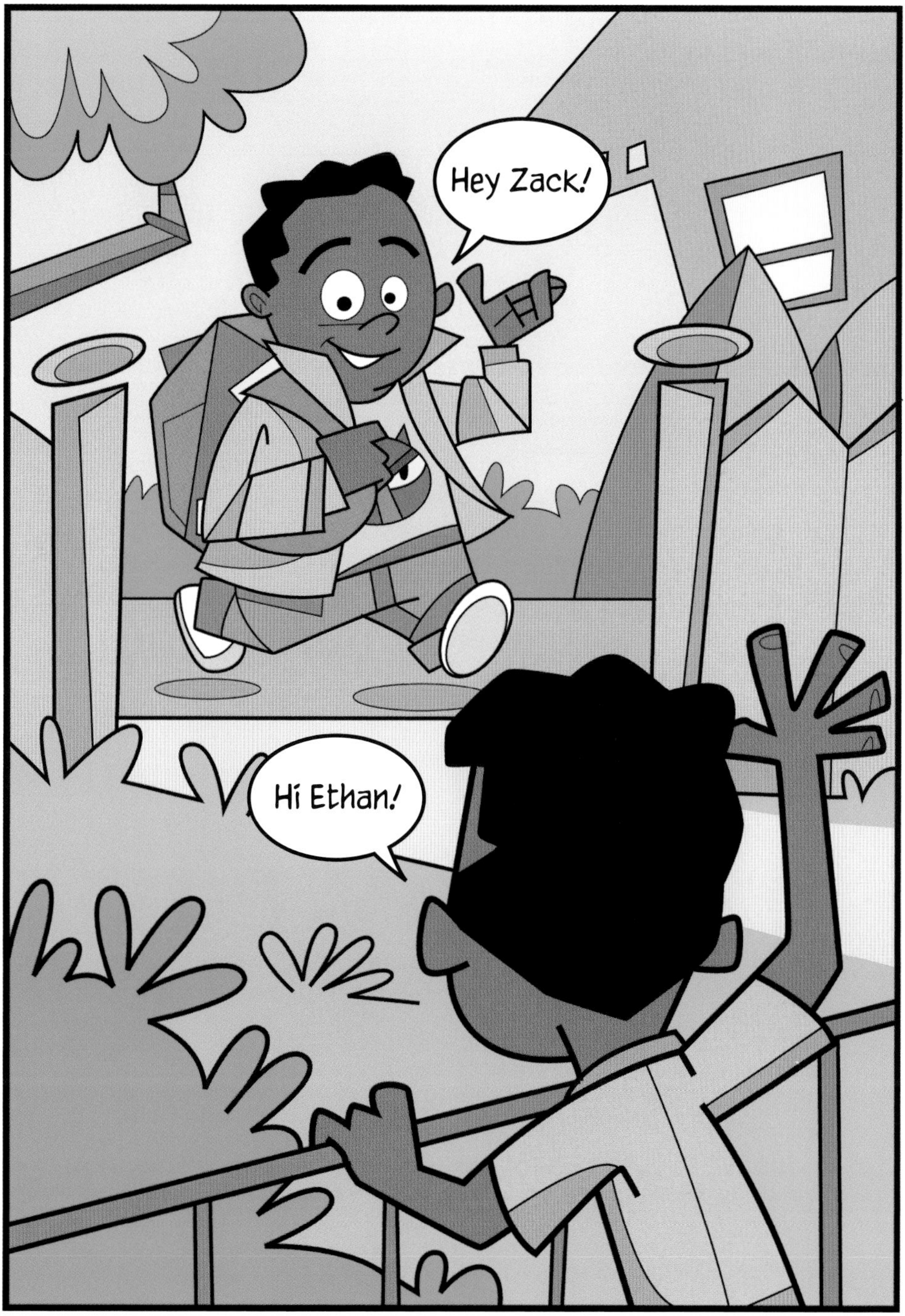
Hey Zack!
Hi Ethan!

Ethan and Zack sat on the floor. They spread out all of their Monster Cards.

Ethan reached inside his pocket. It wasn't there.

Ethan checked his pockets. They were all empty.

Ethan could not find his new card.

They slowly walked back to Ethan's house. Ethan stepped on gum. Zack found an old piece of candy.

Zack also found a penny.

Ethan found food wrappers.

They searched everywhere. They didn't find
Ethan's card.

Ethan went inside and hung up his coat.

Ethan looked under his bed. Zack looked
under the couch cushions.

They both looked in the garbage.

But Ethan's card was gone.

Then Ethan had an idea. He got a pencil and wrote down clues.

He wrote what he had done before he went
to Zack's house.

Ethan raced to the kitchen table. He looked under the newspaper.

But the card wasn't there.

Ethan looked at the clues again. Being a detective was hard work.

Ethan grabbed his brown coat. Something fell out of the pocket.

His new Monster Card was in the pocket of his brown coat, not his blue coat!

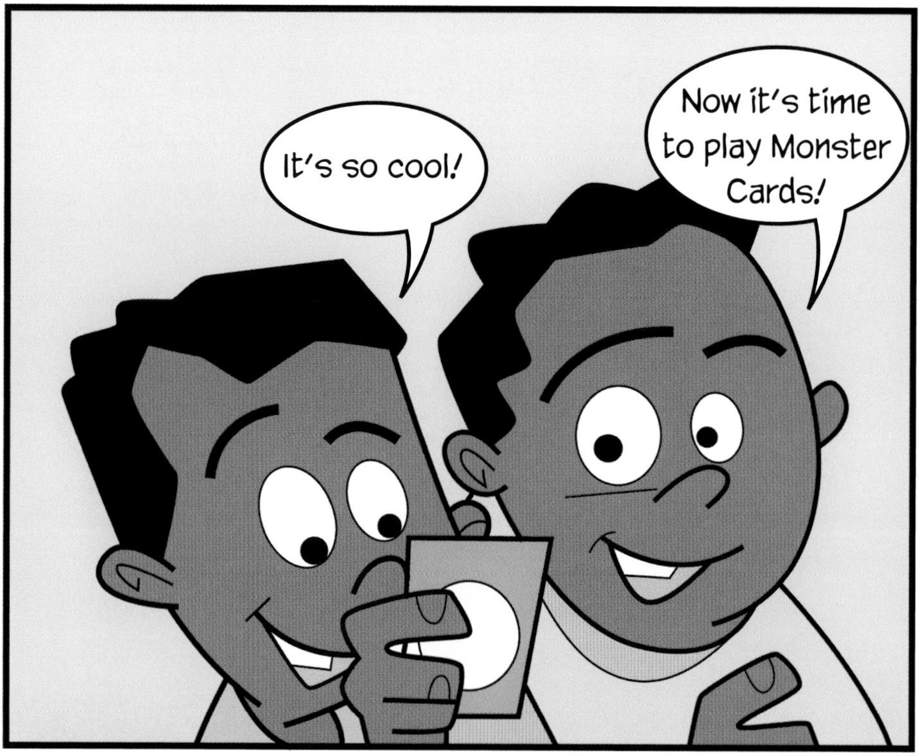
It's so cool!
Now it's time to play Monster Cards!

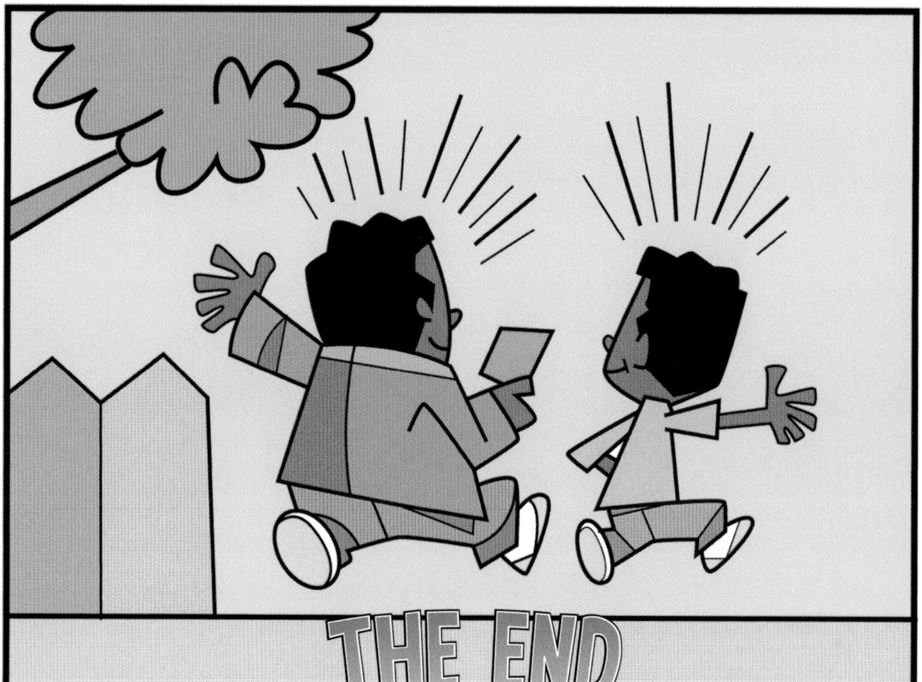
THE END

Lori Mortensen is a multi-published children's author who writes fiction and nonfiction on all sorts of subjects. When she's not plunking away at the keyboard, she enjoys making cheesy bread rolls, gardening, and hanging out with her family at their home in northern California.

Artist Rémy Simard began his career as an illustrator in 1980. Today he creates computer-generated illustrations for a large variety of clients. He has also written and illustrated more than 30 children's books in both French and English, including *Monsieur Noir et Blanc*, a finalist for Canada's Governor's Prize. To relax, Rémy likes to race around on his motorcycle. Rémy resides in Montreal with his two sons and a cat named Billy.

GLOSSARY

CLUES (KLOOZ) — things that help you find the answer to a mystery

DETECTIVES (di-TEK-tivz) — people who try to solve mysteries or crimes

MYSTERY (MISS-tur-ee) — something that is hard to understand or explain

PRICELESS (PRISSE-liss) — so valuable that no amount of money could buy it

SEARCHED (SURCHD) — looked for something

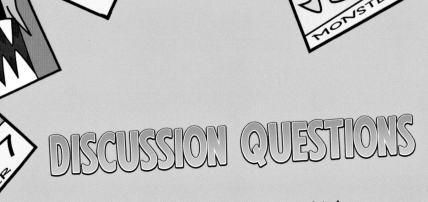

DISCUSSION QUESTIONS

1. Do you have any items that you think are priceless? Discuss what makes these items so special to you.

2. Every Saturday, Zack and Ethan get together to play Monster Cards. Talk about an activity that you would like to do every week.

3. Do you want to be a detective? Why or why not?

WRITING PROMPTS

1. Lots of people collect things. If you had to collect something, what would it be? Write a paragraph about your collection.

2. Pretend you lost the most valuable thing you own. What would you do? Write a paragraph describing your detective plan.

3. Were you able to solve the card mystery? Look through the book again. List any clues you see that would help you solve the mystery.

MY 1ST GRAPHIC NOVEL®

THE 1ST STEP INTO GRAPHIC NOVELS

These books are the perfect introduction to the world of safe, appealing graphic novels. Each story uses familiar topics, repeating patterns, and core vocabulary words appropriate for a beginning reader. Combine the entertaining story with comic book panels, exciting action elements, and bright colors and a safe graphic novel is born.

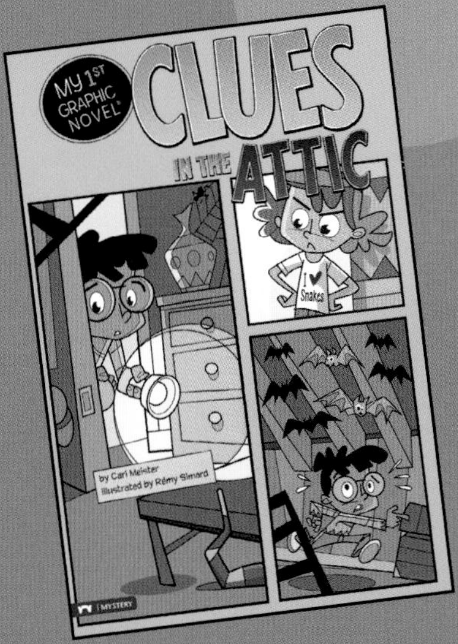
MY 1ST GRAPHIC NOVEL
CLUES IN THE ATTIC
I ♥ Snakes
by Cari Meister
illustrated by Rémy Simard
MYSTERY

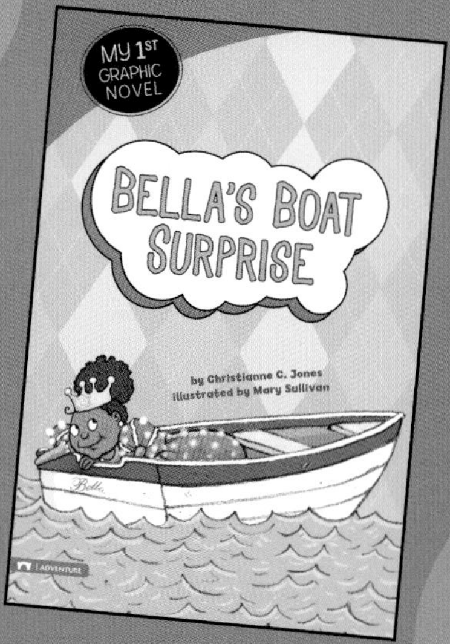
MY 1ST GRAPHIC NOVEL
BELLA'S BOAT SURPRISE
by Christianne C. Jones
illustrated by Mary Sullivan
Bella
ADVENTURE

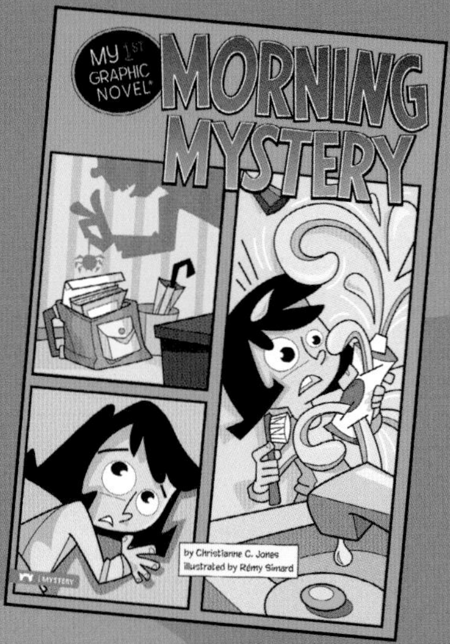
MY 1ST GRAPHIC NOVEL
MORNING MYSTERY
by Christianne C. Jones
illustrated by Rémy Simard
MYSTERY

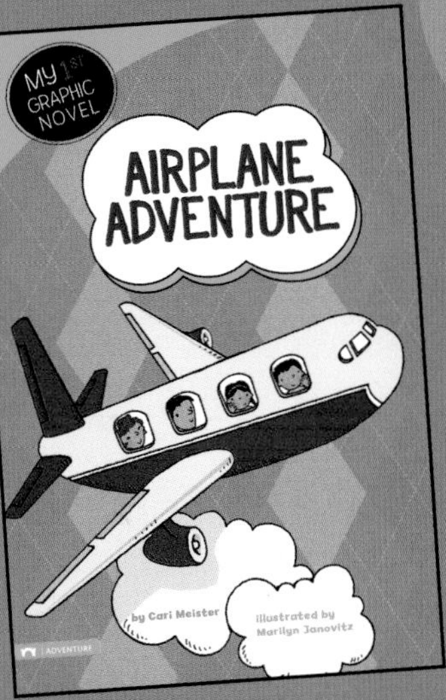
MY 1ST GRAPHIC NOVEL
AIRPLANE ADVENTURE
by Cari Meister
illustrated by Marilyn Janovitz
ADVENTURE

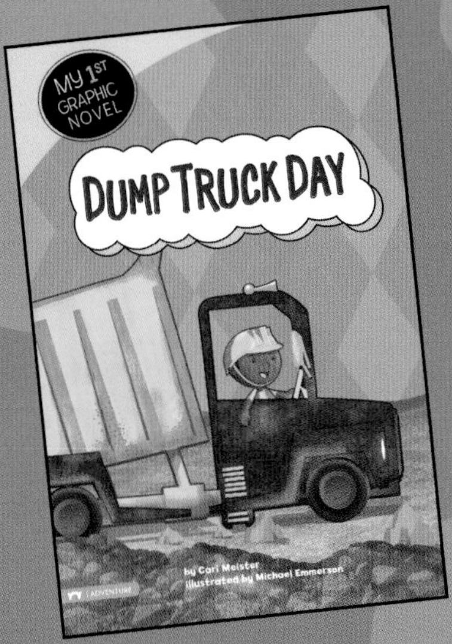
MY 1ST GRAPHIC NOVEL
DUMP TRUCK DAY
by Cari Meister
illustrated by Michael Emmerson
ADVENTURE

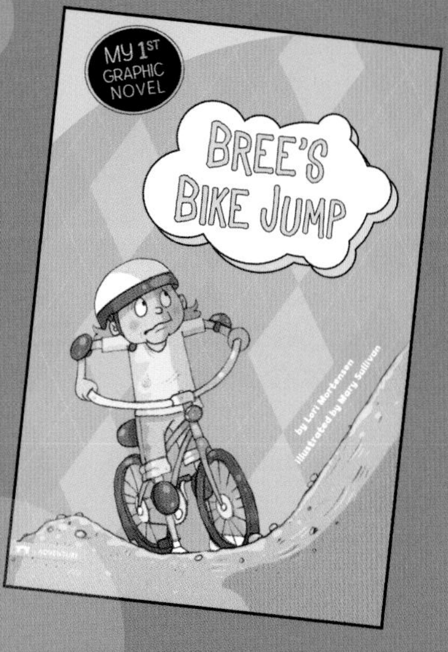
MY 1ST GRAPHIC NOVEL
BREE'S BIKE JUMP
by Lori Mortensen
illustrated by Mary Sullivan
ADVENTURE